Whose
Baby
Am I?

John Butler

Viking

For Lucy

VIKING

Published by the Penguin Group
Penguin Putnam Books for Young Readers, 345 Hudson Street, New York, New York 10014, U.S.A.

Penguin Books Ltd, Registered Offices: 80 Strand, London WC2R 0RL, England

First published in the United States of America by Viking, a division of Penguin Putnam Books for Young Readers, 2001

012 - 12

LIBRARY OF CONGRESS CATALOGING-IN-PUBLICATION DATA
Butler, John, date
Whose baby am I? / John Butler.
p. cm
ISBN-13: 978-0-670-89683-7 (hardcover)
1. Animals—Infancy—Juvenile literature. [1. Animals—Infancy.]
I.Title.
QL763 .B75 2001
591.3'9—dc21
00-011200

Manufactured in China

The art was prepared in acrylic and colored pencil.

Whose baby am I?

I am an owl baby.

Whose baby am I?

I am an elephant baby.

Whose baby am I?

I am a koala baby.

Whose baby am I?

I am a giraffe baby.

Whose baby am I?

I am a seal baby.

Whose baby am I?

I am a panda baby.

Whose baby am I?

I am a zebra baby.

Whose baby am I?

I am a penguin baby.

Whose baby am I?

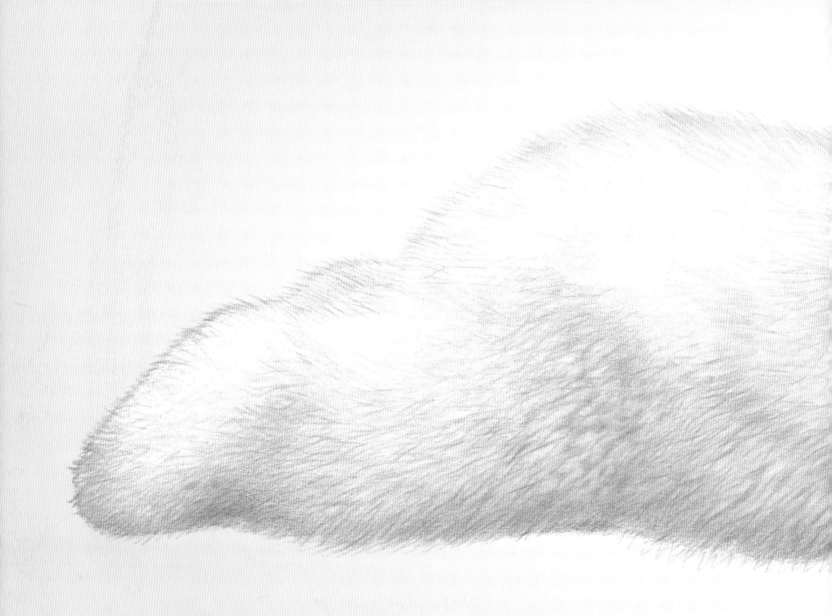

I am a polar bear baby.

Can you guess

whose baby is whose?

Cub

Pup

Calf

Calf

Joey

Owle

Cub

Chick

Foal